A Small Treasury
of

EASTER

Poems and Prayers

Illustrated by Susan Spellman

A Small Treasury
of
EASTER

Poems and Prayers

Illustrated by Susan Spellman

BOYDS MILLS PRESS

Published by Bell Books
Boyds Mills Press, Inc.
A Highlights Company
815 Church Street
Honesdale, Pennsylvania 18431
Printed in Mexico

Publisher Cataloging-in-Publication Data
A small treasury of Easter poems and prayers / illustrated by Susan
Spellman.—1st ed.
[32]p. : col. ill. ; cm.
Summary : A collection of Easter poems for children, both secular and religious.
ISBN 1-56397-647-1
1. Easter—Juvenile Poetry. 2. Easter—Literary collections—Juvenile literature. 3. Prayers—Juvenile literature.
[1. Easter—Poetry. 2. Prayers.] I. Spellman, Susan, ill. II. Title.
808.8/033-dc20   1997   CIP   AC
Library of Congress Catalog Card Number 96-79428

First edition, 1997
Book designed by Tim Gillner
The text of this book is set in 14-point Minion.
The illustrations are done in colored pencil.

10 9 8 7 6 5 4 3 2 1

ACKNOWLEDGEMENTS:

"Easter's Coming" and "Early, Early Easter Day" from *Skip Around the Year* by Aileen Fisher.
Copyright © 1967 by Aileen Fisher. Reprinted by permission. Excerpt from "The Easter
Bunny" by John Ciardi. Copyright © 1985 by John Ciardi. Reprinted by permission of The
Estate of John Ciardi. "Small Surprises" and "Blessings" by Rebecca Kai Dotlich. Copyright
© 1997 by Rebecca Kai Dotlich. Reprinted by permission. "Dream Rabbits" and "Rabbit
Secrets" by Christine San José. Copyright © 1997 by Christine San José. Reprinted by
permission. "The Easter Church," "Easter Skies," and "Easter Prayer" by Lisa Bahlinger.
Copyright © 1997 by Lisa Bahlinger. Reprinted by permission. "Easter Riddles" by Mary
Lou Carney. Copyright © 1988 by Guideposts Associates, Inc. Reprinted by permission. "At
Easter" and "Easter Egg Hunt" by Eileen Spinelli. Copyright © 1997 by Eileen Spinelli.
Reprinted by permission. All other poems copyright © by Highlights for Children, Inc.
All rights reserved.

EASTER IS A TIME FOR PLAY

EASTER IS A TIME TO PRAY

EASTER IS A TIME FOR PLAY

EASTER'S COMING

Through the sunshine,
through the shadow,
down the hillside,
down the meadow,
little streams
run bright and merry,
bursting with news
they carry,
singing, shouting,
laughing, humming,
"Easter's coming,
Easter's coming!"

Aileen Fisher

FROM THE EASTER BUNNY

There once was an egg that felt funny.
It was chocolate brown, and got runny
    When a clucky old hen
    Sat to hatch it, and when
She was done, what popped out was—a bunny!

Said the hen, looking down, "Well, I say!
You're a strange looking chick! But please stay
    Till you learn to say *peep*."
    "There's a date I must keep,"
Said the bunny, and hip-hopped away.

John Ciardi

SMALL SURPRISES

Easter eggs
with swirls and spots,
and brightest yellow
polka dots;
small surprises just for me—
beside the porch,
behind the tree.
Colored eggs
with fine designs,
and pretty purple
squiggly lines.
Palest pink
and darkest blue;
small surprises just for you—

Behind the bush,
beside the gate.
Tucked behind the light,
too late!
By the mailbox—there!
I see one!
Hiding from me,
dipped-in-green one.
Treasures hidden
here
and there.
Enough for
everyone to share.
Easter baskets
in all sizes,
full of lovely *small surprises*!

Rebecca Kai Dotlich

EASTER EGGS

Easter brings so many eggs
In every lovely hue—
Pink and green and yellow,
And some are chocolate, too.

In happy Easter baskets,
Boxes, nests, and hay—
Enough for every boy and girl
To have on Easter Day.

And if you'll look, perhaps you'll see
Beneath a bush, behind a tree,
Beside the swing, upon a ledge,
Or snuggled in the lilac hedge,

The bunnies hopping to-and-fro
As if they wanted you to know
About the eggs they'd tucked away
For you to find on Easter Day.

Grace B. Hilton

SING A SONG OF EASTER

Sing a song of Easter—
  Lilies in a row,
Baskets full of colored eggs
  Everywhere you go.

Sing a song of Easter—
  Joy for everyone,
Cuddly little rabbits
  Frisking in the sun.

Sing a song of Easter—
  Robins in the trees,
Daffodils and jonquils
  Nodding in the breeze.

Sing a song of Easter—
  Church bells in the air,
Happy children's voices
  Ringing everywhere.

    Elizabeth Upham

EASTER EGG HUNT

I found a toad. I found a twig.
I found a poison ivy sprig.
I found a nut. I found a rock.
I even found a dirty sock.
At last—a glimpse of pink. I dashed
to find an egg, but it was smashed.

Eileen Spinelli

EARLY, EARLY EASTER DAY

Easter Day we got up early.
Morning still was gray and pearly,
chimney smoke was not yet curly,
early, early Easter Day.

Out into the dawn we hurried,
up the hill we skipped and scurried.
Would we see it? We were worried.
Would we see it, Easter Day?

We looked east, and just that minute
something round, with crimson in it,
started rising, while a linnet
sang a song on Easter Day.

First the sun was red and flaring,
then it turned all golden-glaring,
as we stood there staring, staring,
early, early Easter Day.

Aileen Fisher

DREAM RABBITS

While I sleep
dream rabbits leap
with mighty midnight hops
across forest tops
over seas at a bound
circling the world around.
I know they'll be
in my yard before day
to hide my Easter eggs away.

Christine San José

At Easter

Daffodils in April's light—
Bloom bright.

Robin on the garden seat—
Sing sweet.

Baby rabbit in your nest—
Be blessed.

World with last year's dreams askew—
All is new.

Eileen Spinelli

RABBIT SECRETS

What do you hear with those ears, rabbit?
What do you smell with that nose?
What do you spy with those bright brown eyes?
What is it your rabbit heart knows?

Do you hear the bells ring far and near, rabbit?
Do you smell new life a-borning?
Do you spy the glory that fills the sky?
Does your heart know it's Easter morning?

Christine San José

EASTER IS A TIME TO PRAY

EASTER SKIES

Still in the hush
the whole night long
God planned
an Easter song.

Then over the hush
came a breath
to fade the dark
to warm and bless.

He is risen!
Let us rise,
to greet the rosy
Easter skies.

Lisa Bahlinger

REJOICE

Bells are ringing far away.
  I like to hear them when they say:
"It's Easter Day, it's Easter Day.
  Rejoice! Rejoice!"

Across the land, bells are ringing,
  The blessed, blessed message bringing,
The church choirs and children singing,
  "Rejoice! Rejoice!"

Edna Hamilton

BLESSINGS

Bless the roosters and the rabbits.
Bless the Easter song we sing.
Bless the lilacs and the lilies;
all the hope that Easter brings.

Bless the jellybeans and chocolate.
Bless our Easter Day parade.
Bless the ducklings and the bunnies;
all the creatures God has made.

Bless the Easter eggs we color.
Bless our Easter baskets, too.
Bless the lovely morning-glories;
all our friends, both old and new.

Bless our fancy Easter bonnets.
Bless our work and bless our play.
Bless our families and each other,
on this blessed Easter Day.

Rebecca Kai Dotlich

EASTER PRAYER

We thank you for the feast that's spread.
Bless this table,
bless this bread,
bless us, Lord,
each bent head.

We thank you for our loved ones dear.
Bless our family
through the years,
and thank you
for your presence here.

Lisa Bahlinger

EASTER MESSAGE

Easter morning bright and fair,
Tells me of God's loving care.
Flowers that were gone from view
Now awakening, bloom anew.

Though God's face I do not see,
I will trust His care for me.

Jennifer Hayden

And they brought the colt to Jesus, and threw their garments on it; and He sat on it. And many spread their garments on the road, and others spread leafy branches, which they had cut from the fields. And those who went before and those who followed cried out, "Hosanna! Blessed is he who comes in the name of the Lord! Blessed is the kingdom of our father David that is coming! Hosanna in the highest!"

Mark 11:7–10

EASTER RIDDLES

I stood there munching
Grass and hay
And bellowing out
An occasional bray.

Then two men came
Took me away.
It turned out to be
An incredible day!

Who am I?

He overturned the tables
Of all who bought and sold.
He quoted Holy Scripture
Penned in days of old.

My tiny cage He shattered
And skyward I did fly.
My wings stretched out in freedom

Now tell me, *who am I?*

I'm a symbol of love and affection
Given to those you hold dear.
Grandmas and grandpas and uncles,
Cousins from far and near.

But Judas, the evildoer,
Used me a different way
That night in the darkened garden
When he the Savior betrayed.

What am I?

We were common criminals
Who both deserved to die.
We had stolen whatever we'd wanted.
Our guilt we couldn't deny.

But the man they hung between us
Was as different as could be.
We paid our debt for our sinful ways.
He died to set men free!

Who are we?

Mary Lou Carney

At Easter Time

The little flowers came through the ground,
  At Easter time, at Easter time:
They raised their heads and looked around,
  At happy Easter time.
And every pretty bud did say,
  "Good people bless this holy day,
For Christ is risen, the angels say,
  At happy Easter time!"

The pure white lily raised its cup
  At Easter time, at Easter time:
The crocus to the sky looked up
  At happy Easter time.
"We'll hear the song of Heaven!" they say,
  "Its glory shines on us today.
Oh! may it shine on us always
  At holy Easter time!"

'Twas long and long and long ago,
  That Easter time, that Easter time:
But still the pure white lilies blow
  At happy Easter time.
And still each little flower doth say
  "Good Christians, bless this holy day,
For Christ is risen, the angels say,
  At blessed Easter time!"

Laura E. Richards

28

A Prayer at Easter

Many, many years ago
  On the shores of Galilee,
Teaching of our Father's love,
  Jesus lived and died for me.

He loved all little children well—
  Set a child upon his knee,
Held it in his arms and said,
  "Let the children come to me."

Heavenly Father of us all
  Help me love most gratefully
All mankind, as Jesus loved,
  For he lived and died for me.

Jennifer Hayden

At that time, Mary Magdalene, Mary the mother of James, and Salome bought spices that they might go and anoint Jesus. And very early on the first day of the week, they came to the tomb, when the sun had just risen. And they were saying to one another, "Who will roll the stone back from the entrance of the tomb for us?" And looking up they saw that the stone had been rolled back, for it was very large. But on entering the tomb, they saw a young man sitting at the right side, clothed in a white robe, and they were amazed. He said to them, "Do not be terrified. You are looking for Jesus of Nazareth, who was crucified. He has risen. He is not here. Behold the place where they laid Him. But go, tell His disciples and Peter that He goes before you into Galilee; there you shall see Him, as He told you."

Mark 16:1–7

THE EASTER CHURCH

Yesterday we were a sad people,
an ashes-to-ashes people,
can't-say-alleluia, gave-it-up-for-Lent people,
　　dull days, blue days,
　　　sad, nothing new days.

　　But today is Easter!
　　Everything has changed:
there are lilies on the altar,
candles shining cold,
baskets of eggs, fragrant breads,
and stories to be told.

Sun shines through the windows
on each warm face: brown, strong,
old, long, pink, tan,
every woman, every man,
children smile, and we all sing,
to thank our God
for everything.

Alleluia!

　　　　Lisa Bahlinger

I am the resurrection, and the life:
he that believeth in me, though he
   were dead, yet shall he live:
And whosoever liveth and believeth
   in me shall never die.
Believest thou this?

John 11:25–26